PEGASUS ENCYCLOPEDIA
FLOODS

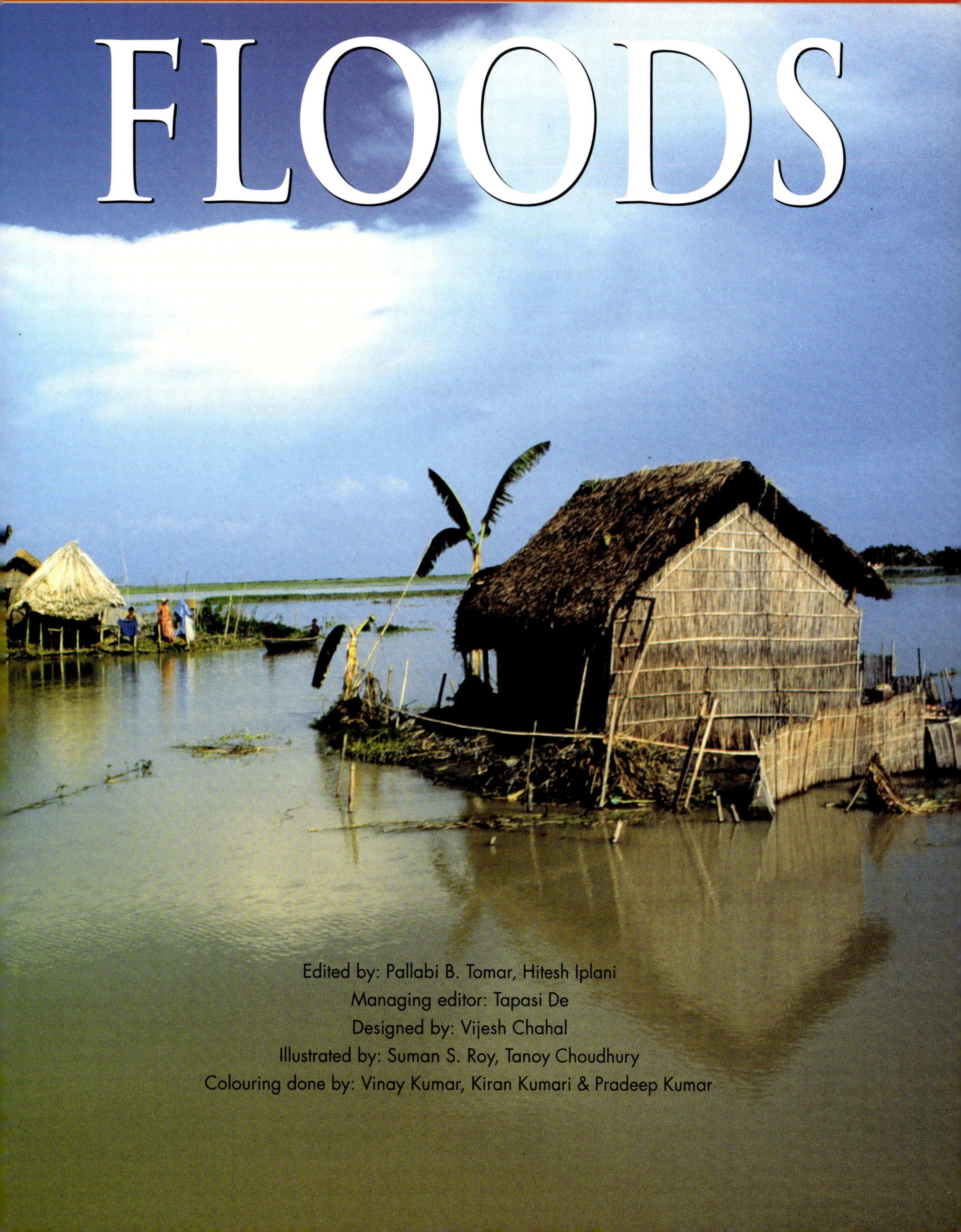

Edited by: Pallabi B. Tomar, Hitesh Iplani
Managing editor: Tapasi De
Designed by: Vijesh Chahal
Illustrated by: Suman S. Roy, Tanoy Choudhury
Colouring done by: Vinay Kumar, Kiran Kumari & Pradeep Kumar

CONTENTS

What is a flood? 3

Causes of floods 5

Types of floods 8

Effects of flood 12

Flood control and prevention 16

Benefits of floods 19

Better safe than sorry 20

Deadliest floods in history 23

Test Your Memory 31

Index 32

What is a flood?

A flood is when the water level in a creek, river, lake or the sea rises and covers land that is usually dry. Floods are caused by many things, including rainstorms, earthquakes, broken dams, underwater volcanic eruptions, tsunamis or hurricanes.

Floods are natural phenomena common in many places around the world where either there is river nearby or the local weather can dump large amounts of rain. The word 'Flood' comes from Old English, *Flod*.

Flooding and flash flooding are the deadliest of natural disasters. Floodwaters claim thousands of lives every year and render millions homeless. One of the more frightening things about flooding is that it can occur nearly anywhere, at any time. It can result from excess water jams in rivers, even moderate rain, or a single very heavy downpour.

Astonishing fact

It is seen that a 'hundred-year flood' is an extremely large, destructive event that happens only once in every century.

FLOODS

People need water to live. The oceans cover three-fourths of Earth, making it the only blue planet in our solar system that can sustain life. We drink it, we bathe in it and we swim in it. 65% of our bodies are composed of water. But when it floods, water has the ability to kill. In fact, most floods cause a lot of damage because they happen so unexpectedly.

Floods bring misery to those that live in the area. They can cause loss of life and often cause a great disruption of daily life. Water can come into people's houses, drinking water and electricity supplies may break down, roads can be blocked and people cannot go to work or to school. Floods all over the world cause enormous damages every year like economic damages, damage to the natural environment and damage to national heritage sites.

Astonishing fact

Did you know that 6 inches of rapidly moving flood water can knock a person down!

Causes of floods

Floods are caused by numerous environmental, seasonal and human factors. All flooding can be dangerous and potentially deadly, although buildings and property damage are among the most common outcomes. Although large-scale floods are thought of as the most dangerous, smaller floods and flash floods can cause much harm as well.

Flood is a common natural disaster brought about by any of the following:

Heavy rainfall raises the water level. When the water level is higher than the river bank or the dams, the water comes out from the river and there is flooding.

Due to global warming, the temperature is higher than the temperature that existed many years ago. The ice caps melt in spring, and the water goes into the sea. The water raises the sea level and makes the river level rise. When river level rises, flooding occurs.

Flooding often occurs in lowlands. This is because rivers flow more slowly in low-lying areas. If the water volume increases suddenly, floods occur.

Astonishing fact

A car can easily be carried away by just 6 m of floodwater.

Flooding always occurs in coastal areas. High tides or storms cause the water level to rise. If the water level is higher than the level of the coastal lowland, flooding will occur.

Deforestation in the uplands can also cause floods. When forests are cleared on mountain slopes and there are no more roots to hold the excess water after a heavy rain, the rapid run-off erodes the topsoil and also floods the land below.

Poor drainage systems in cities and new housing estates where the drains are choked or there are insufficient outlets for the water to drain off after a heavy downpour also cause floods.

Many a time animals too graze much on the land and the pasture is eaten away quickly. Less vegetation results in soil being washed into the rivers easily.

Causes of floods

When a piece of land has been used for farming for a long period of time, the soil may become so infertile that no vegetation can grow on it. As the land becomes less fertile than before, the soil washes into the rivers more easily.

When the dams are poorly constructed or maintained, they can easily collapse and this result in flooding. In China, many lakes along the major rivers have been heavily silted and reclaimed.

Astonishing fact

In United States, floods damage property worth $6 billion and kill about 140 people every year.

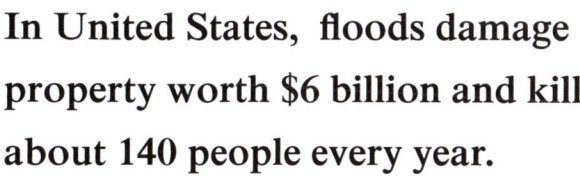

Types of floods

There are four major types of floods: **river floods**, **flash floods**, **coastal floods** and **urban floods**.

River floods

A river flood is one of the most common forms of natural disaster. It occurs when a river fills with water beyond its capacity. The surplus water overflows the banks and runs into the adjoining low-lying lands. River floods are responsible for the loss of human life and the damage of property. Each year, the number of deaths from flooding of rivers is more than any other natural disaster.

Several factors can cause a river flood. The most common reason of river flooding is heavy rainfall. The sudden melting of snow and ice also increases the chance of flooding. Other causes of river floods include broken dams, rough seas and high tides. These events can push water up the rivers and result in flooding.

Astonishing fact

A mere 6 m of water can float even a bus!

Types of floods

Flash floods

A flash flood is the fastest-moving type of flood. It happens when heavy rain collects in a stream or gully, turning the normally calm area into an instant rushing current. The quick change from calm to a raging river is what catches people off guard making flash floods very dangerous.

Any flood involves water rising and overflowing its normal path. But a flash flood is a specific type of flood that appears and moves quickly across the land, with little warning that it is coming.

Many things can cause a flash flood. Generally, they are the result of heavy rainfall concentrated over one area. Most flash flooding is caused by slow-moving thunderstorms that repeatedly move over the same area or heavy rains from hurricanes and tropical storms. Dam failures can create the worst flash flood events. When a dam or levee breaks, a gigantic quantity of water is suddenly let loose downstream, destroying anything in its path.

Flash flood waters move at very fast speeds. They have the power to move boulders, tear out trees, destroy buildings, and demolish bridges. Walls of water can reach heights of 3-6 m and generally carry a huge amount of debris with them.

The best response to any signs of flash flooding is to move immediately and quickly to a higher ground.

> **Surveys reveal that more than 70,000 Americans become shelterless due to flash floods and more than 120 individuals are killed in a year.**

FLOODS

Coastal floods

The earth has seven oceans that cover almost three-fourths of its surface. Naturally, wind and other factors cause ocean water to sometimes overflow. When this happens, flooding on the shores occurs. Ocean storms can dump lots of water on a coast, raising the sea level in that area. These are known as storm surges and cause coastal flooding.

Coastal flooding usually occurs as a result of severe storms, either tropical or winter storms. Ocean waves intensify on the open ocean and these storms make surface water much fierce than normal. Raging winds can create huge waves that crash on beaches.

Hurricanes and tropical storms can produce heavy rains, or drive ocean water onto land. Beaches and coastal houses can be swept away by the water. Coastal flooding can also be produced by sea waves called tsunamis, giant tidal waves that are created by volcanoes or earthquakes in the ocean.

Astonishing fact

Flash floods often bring walls of water which are 3-6 m high!

Types of floods

Urban floods

Urban floods are floods that happen in a relatively short period of time and can submerge an area with several metres of water. In most of the urban areas, roads are usually paved. With heavy rain, the large amount of rain water cannot be absorbed into the ground and leads to urban floods. The main problem with urban flooding is the fact that they occur in highly populated areas.

Urban floods are when land is converted from fields or woodlands to roads and parking lots; it loses it ability to absorb rainfall. Urbanization increases runoff two to six times over what would occur in natural terrain. During urban flooding, streets can become swift moving rivers, while basements can become deadly as they fill with water.

In addition to the increase in urban structures, there is a resultant decrease in vegetation. Trees, shrubs, and grasses cannot take away some of the water that enters into an area as a result of the water cycle.

Astonishing fact

The great Mississippi River Flood of 1993 covered an area which was 800 km long and 321 km wide. More than 50,000 homes were damaged, and 19,312 km of farmland were washed out.

11

FLOODS

Effects of flood

Floods are one of the most widespread and destructive natural disasters occurring due to various reasons like heavy rainfall, damming of rivers, hurricanes and melting of snow. Often floods are sudden and are difficult to predict. Floods occurring in densely populated urban areas have the capacity to do maximum damage to life and property.

The major effects of floods are destruction of life and property. Each year thousands of people lose their lives due to floods and millions are rendered homeless. In areas where there are no measures to predict occurrence of floods and to evacuate people to safety, the loss of life and damage to property is maximum.

Flooding causes damage to infrastructures like roads and bridges in urban areas and destroys farmlands in agricultural areas. The sewerage systems are often submerged due to floods resulting in the overflowing of drains. The accumulation of water in pools results in spread of various infectious diseases.

Effects of flood

The effects of flood damage can be categorized into three types, namely, **primary**, **secondary** and **tertiary**.

The primary effects of flood damage includes physical damages like damage to bridges, cars, buildings, sewer systems, roadways and even casualties like people and livestock death due to drowning. The primary effect of floods is due to direct contact with the flood waters. The velocity of water tends to be high in floods and consequently, discharge increases as velocity increases. Due to excess rainfall, the rivers and streams flow with higher velocities wherein they are able to transport larger particles like rocks as suspended load. Such large particles include not only rocks and sediment but during a flood it could also include large objects such as automobiles, houses and bridges. Massive amounts of erosion during the floods can undermine bridge structures, levees and buildings causing their collapse.

> The Yangtze River in China frequently overflows its banks and fills huge plains with large amounts of water, causing catastrophic flooding. There are floods every year during the June-to-September monsoon season. On average at least several hundred people are killed in Yangtze River floods every year.

FLOODS

Secondary effects are those that occur because of the primary effects. Among the secondary effects of a flood are:

Astonishing fact

The Yangtze is responsible for 70 to 75 percent of China's floods. Floods in this river in the 20th century alone have killed more than 300,000 people!

• Drinking water supplies may become polluted, especially if sewerage treatment plants are flooded. This may result in disease and other health effects, especially in under developed countries.

• Gas and electrical service maybe disrupted.

• Transportation systems maybe disrupted, resulting in shortages of food and clean-up supplies. In under developed countries food shortages often lead to starvation.

Effects of flood

Tertiary effects of flood are generally long-term effects.

- Location of river channels may change as the result of flooding; new channels develop, leaving the old channels dry
- Sediment deposited by flooding may destroy farm lands
- Jobs maybe lost due to the disruption of services, destruction of business, etc
- Corruption may result from misuse of relief funds
- Destruction of wildlife habitat

There were catastrophic floods on the Yangtze in 1931, 1935, 1954 and 1998. Over 2,000 are believed to have died in the flood of 1991. Some 4,100 died in the floods in 1998.

Flood control and prevention

Floods are one of the major natural calamities which take a big toll of human life and property. Frequently occurring floods take away million tones of fertility from soil. The method of preventing and reducing the effects of flood water is known as **flood control**.

In China, where most flooding occurs when the Yellow or Yangtze River overflows, people have tried to maintain control by building higher levees, dredging, digging channels and building dams. The work has paid off, for the progress in the last 50 years seems to have stopped serious flooding from the Yellow River. However, the river may still overflow and cause much destruction.

Experts are also warning people not to build in high flood risk areas. However, many people continue to live next to the coast, by rivers and streams or in the middle of wetlands.

Astonishing fact

The Rapid City Flood of 1972 was one of the deadliest floods in US history. More than 200 people lost their lives in a period of hours on the night of June 9-10, 1972.

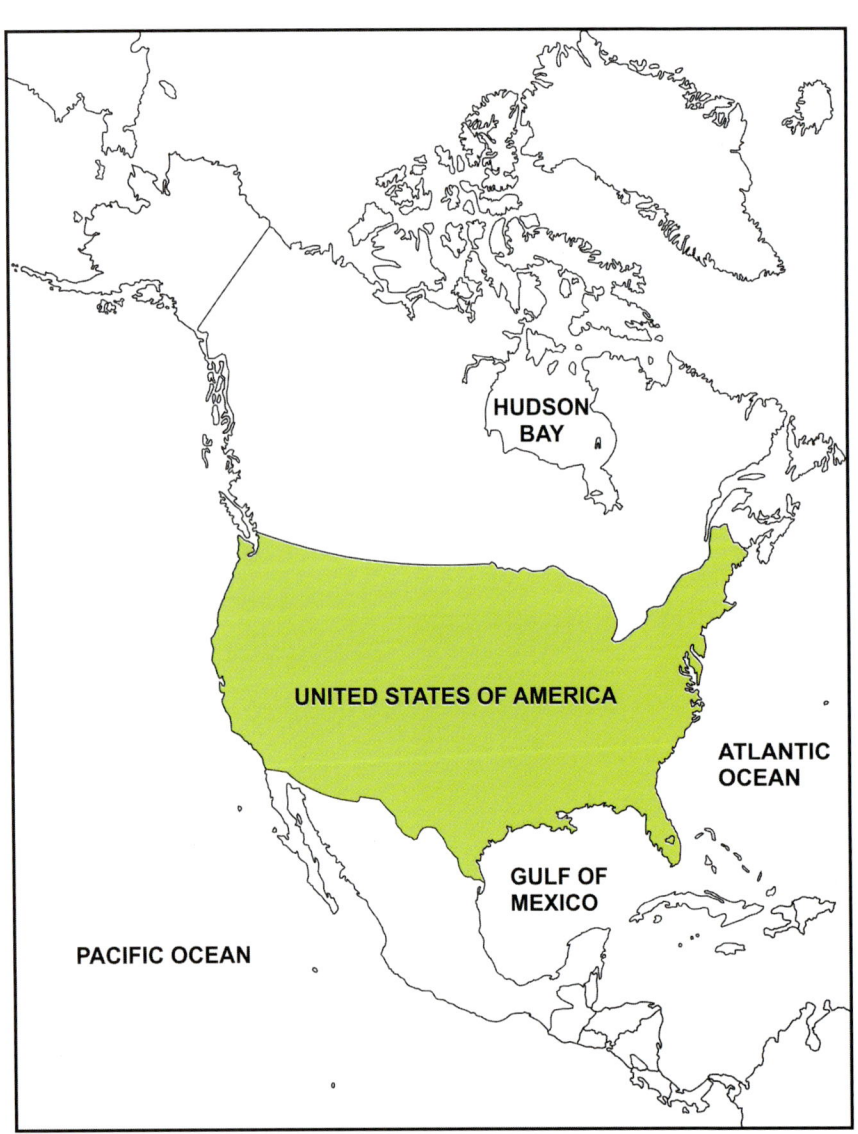

Flood control and prevention

Prevention of flood

There are a myriad of ways to prevent floods. The creation of flood plains and winding streams are two of the best ways to hinder the accumulation of water by providing a route for the drainage of water. Also, the protection of wetlands helps to maintain a natural drainage system to provide a place for the excess water to gather. Such devices allow the water to evaporate before it can accumulate, creating flooding conditions.

Levees also impede the collecting of water. Levees are embankments composed of soil and earthen material that are used to prevent annual flooding in many areas. With a levee, a huge amount of rain water is required before flooding occurs. However, one drawback to their use is that if the water is able to get past the levees, then the flooding is significantly worse and causes several times more damage.

> **Many cultures have ancient flood stories such as the story of Noah or Gilgamesh. One theory suggests that these floods could have been caused by the melting of ice from the last ice age around 12,000 years ago.**

FLOODS

A **dam** is a common flood prevention structure. It blocks water flow from reaching certain areas and collects the water in a reservoir. Dams hold water in a tank, impeding its regular flow. In addition to flood control, dams and reservoirs can aid in drought relief. A dam constructed on a water body's headwaters retains heavy runoff during extreme wet periods. The community can then release this stored runoff water during dry periods.

Reforestation, contouring plowing and crop rotation provide the most common flood prevention techniques in agricultural areas. These combat the damage wrought by the combination of deforestation and over cultivation that results in soil erosion.

> **The Greek flood myth says that Zeus, father of the gods, sent a mighty deluge to destroy the human race.**

Benefits of floods

- Environmentally floods can be important to local ecosystems. Some river floods bring nutrients to soil. A classic example is the Nile River in Egypt that would flood every year and bring nutrients.

- Floods contribute to the health of wetlands.

- Floods distribute rich sediment and refresh streams.

- Allowing rivers and streams to overflow their banks naturally can prevent more serious flooding downstream.

> Several groups among the Aborigines, the native people of Australia believe that a vast flood swept away a previous society. Perhaps these myths grew out of conditions at the end of the last Ice Age, when sea levels rose and coastal regions were flooded.

FLOODS

Better safe than sorry

Flood safety tips

No matter how powerful, people cannot control nature. Tropical storms, hurricanes, thunderstorms and melting snow will cause floods. People with homes in low-lying places, by rivers, or in coastal regions are in danger of being wiped out by floods. To survive, keep your cool and prepare yourself with the supplies and knowledge necessary for survival.

Do not walk through flowing water

Drowning is the number one cause of flood deaths. Most occur during flash floods. Six inches of moving water can knock you off your feet. Use a pole or stick to make sure that the ground is still there before you go through an area where the water is not flowing.

Do not drive through a flooded area

Most people drown in their cars than anywhere else. Don't drive around road barriers; the road or bridge may be washed out.

Stay away from power lines and electrical wires

Electrocution is also a major killer in floods. Electrical current can travel through water.

Astonishing fact

Some floods are so rare that they occur only every 500 years.

Better safe than sorry

Turn off electricity when you return home

Some appliances, such as television sets, can shock you even after they have been unplugged. Don't use appliances or motors that have gotten wet unless they have been taken apart, cleaned and dried.

Watch for animals

Small animals that have been flooded out of their homes may seek shelter in yours. Use a pole or stick to poke and turn items over and scare away small animals.

Look before you step

After a flood, the ground and floors are covered with debris including broken bottles and nails. Floors and stairs that have been covered with mud can be very slippery.

Astonishing fact

Some scientists think that Mars could have had floods only 10 million years ago. That's recent in geologic terms: Mars is probably over 4 billion years old.

Be alert for gas leaks

Use a flashlight to inspect for damage. Don't use candles, lanterns, or open flames unless you are sure that the gas has been turned off and the area has been aired out.

Clean everything wet

Floodwaters pick up sewage and chemicals from roads, farms, factories, and storage buildings. Spoiled food and flooded cosmetics and medicines are health hazards. When in doubt, throw them out.

Take good care

Recovering from a flood is a big job. It is tough on both the body and the spirit. And the effects a disaster has on you and your family may last a long time. Learn how to recognize and care for anxiety, stress, and fatigue.

> **The basic flood myth in which the flood was sent as a divine punishment, originated among the Sumerian cities in southern Mesopotamia. Over a period of several thousand years, the Babylonians, the Hebrews, and other civilizations have developed their own versions.**

Deadliest floods in history

China Floods (1931)

During the later half of 1931, Central China suffered what is considered the most catastrophic flood in recent recorded history. It is generally considered the deadliest natural disaster ever recorded, and certainly the deadliest of the 20th century. Estimates of human death range from 1.3 to 4 million people. In addition to the drowning deaths, many died from disease, starvation, and other by-products of the disaster.

The weather leading up to the floods was exceedingly dry. In fact, the entire region had been plagued with drought from 1928 to 1930. This changed in late 1930 when heavy rains were followed by heavy snows and then further complicated with heavier rains in the spring of 1931.

Combined with the thaw of the snow, the rains caused three of the major Chinese rivers to flood. Besides this, seven cyclones struck the area in July. This was unheard of as the average number of cyclones for an entire season is only two.

The Huang Ho River alone completely flooded 20 million acres and partially covered another five million. This caused between one and two million deaths and 80 million without homes, food or sources of income.

During July and August the Yangtze River area received over 24 inches of rain. The Huai River also flooded. It exceeded 16 m past the normal stage. The combination of the two rivers flooding at the same time left the then Chinese capital Nanjing isolated.

FLOODS

Huang Ho or the Yellow River, China (1887)

The 1887 Yellow River flood was a devastating one in China. This river is prone to flooding due to the elevated nature of the river, running between dykes above the broad plains surrounding it. The flood that began in September 1887 devastated the area, killing some 900,000 people. It was one of the deadliest natural disasters ever recorded.

For centuries, the farmers living near the Yellow River had built dikes to contain the rising waters, caused by silt accumulation on the riverbed. In 1887, this rising riverbed, coupled with days of heavy rain, overcame the dikes on around September 28, causing a massive flood.

The waters of the Yellow River are generally thought to have broken through the dikes in Huayuankou, near the city of Zhengzhou in Henan province. Owing to the low-lying plains near the area, the flood spread very quickly throughout Northern China, covering an estimated 129,499 square km, swamping agricultural settlements and commercial centres. After the flood, two million were left homeless. The resulting pandemic and lack of basic essentials claimed as many lives as those lost directly by the flood itself.

Deadliest floods in history

Ru River, Banqiao Dam, China

The largest, most devastating dam failure was the failure of the Banqiao and Shimantan Reservoir Dams in China in 1975.

This flood was caused by the collapse of the Banquia Dam, along with several others, following a heavy rain caused by a typhoon. It is the worst dam related collapse in history.

The resulting flood waters caused a large wave, which was 10 kilometres wide and 3–7 meters high in Suiping, to rush downwards into the plains below at nearly 50 km per hour, almost wipe out an area 55 km long and 15 kilometres wide, and create temporary lakes as large as 12,000 square km. Seven county seats, namely Suiping, Xiping, Ru'nan, Pingyu, Xincai, Luohe, Linquan, were inundated, as were thousands of square kilometres of countryside and countless communities. Evacuation orders had not been fully delivered because of weather conditions and poor communications. Telegraphs failed, signal flares fired by Unit 34450 were misunderstood, telephones were rare, and some messengers were caught by the flood. While only 827 out of 6,000 people died in the evacuated community of Shahedian just below Banqiao Dam, half of a total of 36,000 people died in the unevacuated Wencheng commune of Suipin County next to Shahedian, and the Daowencheng Commune was wiped from the map, killing all 9,600 citizens. Tens of thousands of them were carried by the water to downriver provinces and many others fled from their homes. Around 90,000-230,000 people were killed as a result of the dam breaking.

FLOODS

Huang He (Yellow) River, China (1938)

The 1938 Yellow River flood was a flood created by the Nationalist Government in central China during the early stage of the Anti-Japanese War in an attempt to halt the rapid advance of the Japanese forces. The floodwaters began pouring out from Huayuankou in the early morning on June 9, 1938. As a result, the course of the Yellow River was diverted southwards for nine years afterward, inundating 54,000 km of land in Henan, Anhui, and Jiangsu provinces. All in all, in an instant after the river had been diverted, the flood waters took an estimated 500,000 to 900,000 lives. It is still debated whether it was necessary to destroy the dike in Huayuankou to cause the flood. Militarily, it is claimed that the strategy could be considered partly successful as the Japanese were essentially in a draw with the Chinese forces by 1940 and because the flood had created 'problems for the mobility of the Japanese Army'. Politically, not much is known of Japan's government's stance towards the Chinese Nationalist government's decision regarding both the attack and lack of evacuation of the mass public in China.

Deadliest floods in history

Kaifeng Flood, China (1642)

Kaifeng, a city in eastern Henan province, People's Republic of China, located along the southern bank of the Yellow River, was flooded during a siege in 1642 by the Ming Dynasty army and by the peasant rebels led by Li Zicheng with water from the Yellow River. Over 300,000 of the 378,000 residents of Kaifeng were killed by the flood and the ensuing disasters such as famine and plague.

The flood is sometimes referred to as a natural disaster due to the role of the Huang He river and is currently listed as the 7th deadliest natural disaster in history with a death toll of some 300,000.

The city was once the capital of China, and after this disaster the city was abandoned until 1662 when it was rebuilt under the rule of the celebrated Qing emperor Kangxi. It remained a rural backwater city of diminished importance thereafter and experienced several other less devastating floods.

Astonishing fact

66 percent of flood deaths occur in vehicles and most happen when drivers make a single, fatal mistake trying to navigate through flood waters.

St. Lucia's Flood

St. Lucia's flood was a storm tide that affected the Netherlands and Northern Germany on December 14, 1287 (the day after St. Lucia Day) when a dike broke during a storm, killing approximately 50,000 to 80,000 people in the fifth largest flood in recorded history. Much land was permanently flooded in what is now the Waddenzee and Ijsselmeer. It especially affected the north of the Netherlands, particularly Friesland. The city of Griend was almost completely destroyed; only ten houses were left standing. The name Zuiderzee dates from this event, as the water had merely been a shallow inland lake when the first dikes were being built, but rising North Sea levels created the 'Southern Sea' when floods including this flood came in.

Deadliest floods in history

Johnstown Pennsylvania Flood

The South Fork Dam collapsed on May 31, 1889, causing a flood in Johnstown, Pennsylvania, that killed more than 2,200 people. In lives lost, the Johnstown Flood was the worst civil disaster the United States ever suffered. On May 31, 1889, after days of rain, the South Fork Dam collapsed and unleashed 20 million tons of water from its reservoir. A wall of water, reaching up to 21 m high, swept 22 km down the Little Conemaugh River Valley, carrying away steel mills, houses, livestock and people. At 4:07 p.m., the floodwaters rushed into the industrial city of Johnstown, crushing houses and downtown businesses in a whirlpool that lasted 10 minutes.

The water flowed through the arches of the Pennsylvania Railroad's stone bridge. The bridge stopped tons of wooden debris, which accumulated in a huge pile that trapped dozens of survivors.

FLOODS

Pakistan floods (2010)

The summer of 2010 produced Pakistan's worst flooding in 80 years. The United Nations estimates that more than 21 million people are injured or homeless as a result of the flooding, exceeding the combined total of individuals affected by the 2004 Indian Ocean tsunami, the 2005 Kashmir earthquake and the 2010 Haiti earthquake.

Flooding began on July 22, 2010, in the province of Baluchistan. The swollen waters then poured across the Khyber-Pakhtunkhwa Province in the northwest before flowing south into Punjab and Sindh. Present estimates indicate that over two thousand people have died and over a million homes have been destroyed since the flooding began.

The flooding, which began with the arrival of the annual monsoons, has affected more than one-fifth of the country — nearly 160,579 square km — or an area larger than England, according to the United Nations.

The floods have damaged millions of hectares of cultivatable land and crops, and many farmers have lost their seeds. And at least 1.2 million livestock have died, crippling poor families who depend on them for food. The government estimates the country has suffered up to $43 billion in damage.

Test Your MEMORY

1. What is a flood?
2. Mention two causes of floods.
3. Write two types of floods.
4. Write a few lines about flash floods.
5. Write about two effects of floods.
6. What is flood control?
7. Write three flood prevention methods.
8. Write two benefits of floods.
9. Write four flood safety tips.
10. Which flood is known as the most devastating flood of the 20th Century?
11. Which flood is listed as the 7th deadliest natural disaster in history?
12. When did the Johnstown Pennsylvania Flood happen?

Index

C

catastrophic 13, 15, 23
coastal areas 6
coastal floods 8

D

dam 9, 18, 25
dams 3, 5, 7, 8, 16, 18
deadliest 3, 16, 23, 24, 27, 31
deforestation 6
destruction 12, 15, 16
destruction 15
dike 26, 28
disease 14, 23
drainage 6, 17
dredging 16

drowning 20

E

electrocution 20

F

flash floods 5, 8, 9, 20, 31
flod 3
flooding 3, 5, 6, 12, 30

G

global warming 5

H

Huai River 23

L

levees 13, 16, 17
lowlands 5

N

natural disasters 3, 12, 24

R

rainstorms 3
reforestation 18
river floods 8, 19

S

sewerage 12, 14
starvation 14, 23

U

urban floods 8, 11

Y

Yangtze River 13, 16, 23